Beth froze with fear. All she could do was stare at the sharp antlers.

Patrick's heart all but stopped. The animals were coming too fast. There were so many of them. It would be useless to run.

Whoosh! A spear came flying through the air.

Thud! It landed right in front of Patrick.

"Where did that come from?" Patrick shouted.

"Who cares?" Beth shouted back at him. "Use it!"

Praise for Voyage with the Vikings

I want to know who Albert is. I want . . . more of these books.

— Taylor, age 8 • Torrance, California

We study the Vikings in our curriculum. These books will help my kids enjoy history. I can't wait for the book on Rome.

— Beth S., third-grade public school teacher
Colorado Springs, Colorado

Voyage with the Vikings taught me that when you face your fears, it will turn out better.

—Rachel, age 9 • Eldersburg, Maryland

Voyage with the Vikings

BOOK 1

Other books in this series

Attack at the Arena
Peril in the Palace
Revenge of the Red Knight
Giant Trouble

Voyage with the Vikings

BOOK 1

MARIANNE HERING • PAUL McCUSKER
ILLUSTRATED BY DAVID HOHN

FOCUS ON THE FAMILY • ADVENTURES IN ODYSSEY
TYNDALE HOUSE PUBLISHERS, INC. • CAROL STREAM, ILLINOIS

Voyage with the Vikings

ISBN: 978-1-58997-664-1

A Focus on the Family book published by Tyndale House Publishers, Inc., Carol Stream, Illinois 60188

Cover design by Michael Heath | Magnus Creative

Library of Congress Cataloging-in-Publication Data

Hering, Marianne.
Voyage with the Vikings / by Marianne Hering and Paul McCusker ; illustrated by David Hohn.
p. cm. -- (Imagination Station ; bk. #1)
"Focus on the Family."
"Adventures in Odyssey."
ISBN 978-1-58997-664-1 (alk. paper)
[1. Space and time--Fiction. 2. Vikings--Fiction. 3. Cousins--Fiction. 4. Christian life--Fiction. 5. Eric, the Red, fl. 985--Fiction. 6. Ericson, Leif, d. ca. 1020--Fiction. 7. Greenland--History--To 1500--Fiction.] I. McCusker, Paul, 1958- II. Hohn, David, 1974- ill. III. Title.
PZ7.H4312580Voy 2010
[Fic]--dc22

2010031142

Printed in the United States of America
1 2 3 4 5 6 7 8 9/ 15 14 13 12 11 10

For manufacturing information regarding this product, please call 1-800-323-9400.

To Joey, Johnny, Justin, Kendrick, Marshall, and Nicholas—six would-be Leif Erikssons

Contents

Whit's End

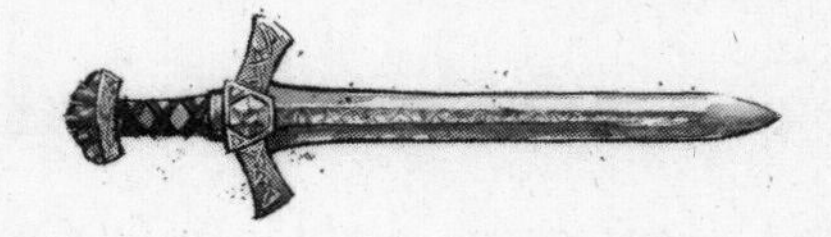

It all began on a Monday.

Beth and her cousin Patrick were at Whit's End. It was a soda shop in a large, old house. Kids thought Whit's End was the best place in town for ice cream.

But there was a lot more to Whit's End than scoops and cones. It had more rooms than Patrick could count.

Down the hallway was a radio studio. And a theater to perform plays. Plus a library.

On the second floor, there was a large model train. And the Bible Room. It was like a kids' museum.

Patrick followed Beth from room to room with wide eyes.

"Are there any video games?" Patrick asked. "The kind with sword fighters? Or guys who fight monsters?"

"No," Beth said. "But I'll show you the Imagination

Station. It's kind of like a time machine."

Patrick liked the words *imagination* and *time machine.*

"Where is it?" Patrick asked.

"It's usually in the corner of the Bible Room," Beth said. "But it's not there today. Come on. Let's ask Mr. Whittaker. Someone said he's in his basement workshop."

Patrick followed Beth down the

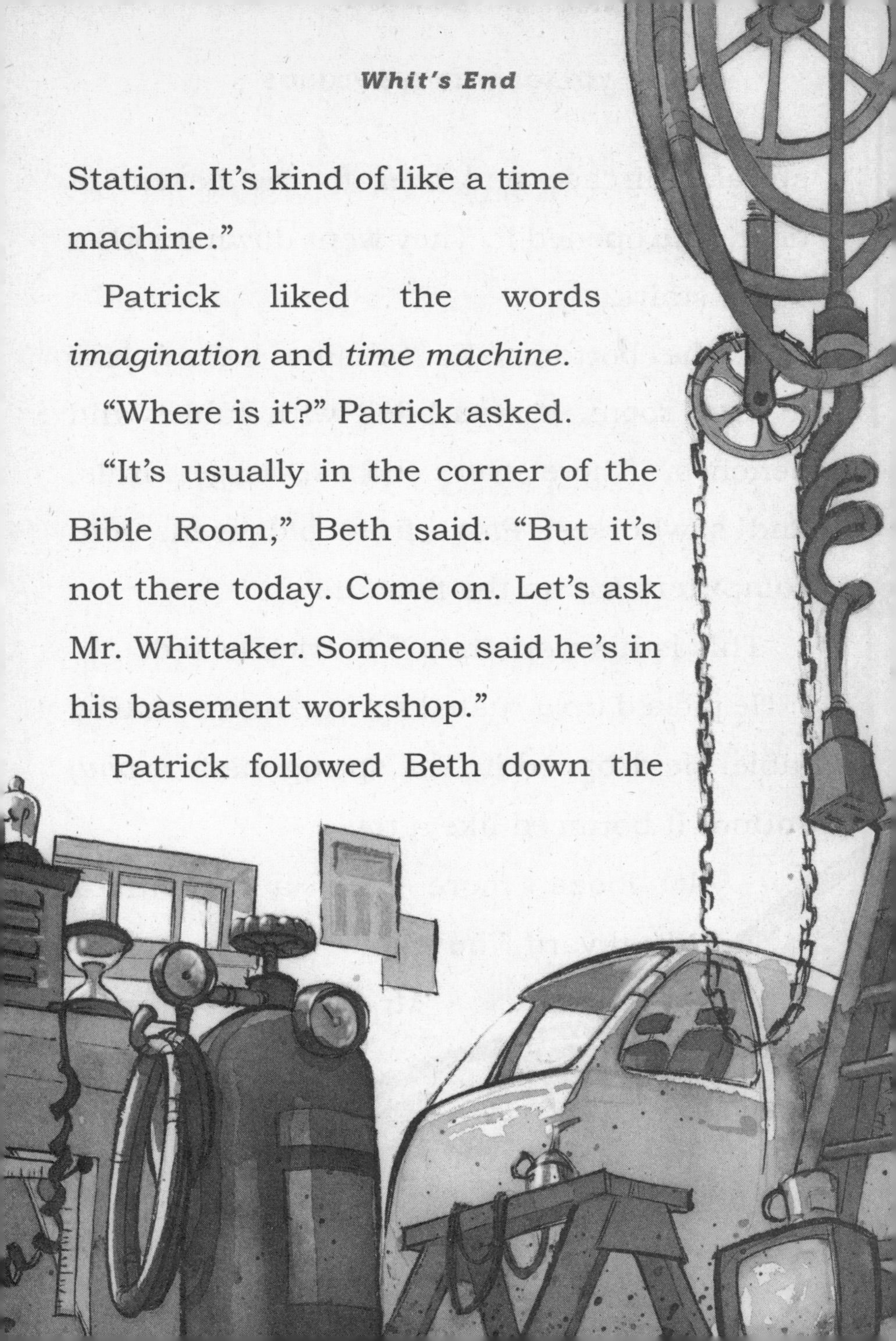

spiral staircase and over to the basement door. She opened it. They went down another set of stairs.

At the bottom, the cousins looked into a large room. It was filled with tables and benches. There were boxes, large drills, and sawhorses. Parts from old ovens and computers sat on the floor.

"This is his workshop?" Patrick asked.

He picked up a rusted spring from a nearby table. He dropped it. The spring made a *ping* sound. It bounced like a toy.

"It looks more like a scientist's junkyard," he said.

"Mr. Whittaker invents things," Beth said.

Beth picked up the spring. She put it back on a table.

Just then Mr. Whittaker came around a corner. He was tall with white hair and a moustache. He also had a kind smile.

"Good morning, Beth," Mr. Whittaker said.

"Hi, this is my cousin Patrick. He's my age," she said. "His mom is my dad's sister."

"Hi," Patrick said.

Suddenly Beth said, "There it is!"

She walked over to a large machine. The front part was round like a helicopter.

"I wanted Patrick to see the Imagination Station," she said.

Mr. Whittaker said, "I'm sorry. It's not working. That's why I brought it down here."

"May we sit in it?" Beth asked.

"Sure," Mr. Whittaker said.

Beth waved for Patrick to join her. She climbed onto the seat. Patrick followed her.

"Look at all these buttons!" he said.

He pointed to a long dashboard. It had lots of buttons, dials, and numbers on it. There was also a piece of paper sitting on the dash.

"Too bad it's not working," Beth said.

"What does this button do?" Patrick asked. He tapped a large red button with his finger.

The machine came alive. A low hum came from the back of the machine. Lights and buttons blinked on the dashboard. Needles on round dials swung back and forth.

"That's very strange," Mr. Whittaker said. "Come out again."

The cousins obeyed. The machine went dark.

Mr. Whittaker climbed inside. He pushed buttons. Nothing happened. He got out again.

"I don't know what's wrong," he said. "It's working for you, but not for me."

"May we try again?" Patrick asked.

"Go ahead," said Mr. Whittaker.

The kids got into the machine. It lit up again. Mr. Whittaker rubbed his chin slowly. He looked puzzled.

"It wants to take us for a ride!" Patrick said.

"May we go?" Beth asked. "Please?"

The Costume Closet

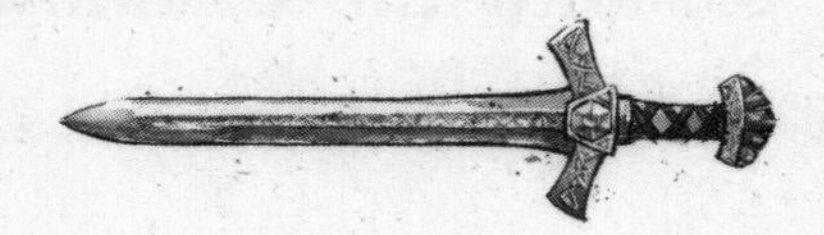

Mr. Whittaker walked over to a computer table. Beth and Patrick watched as he typed some things on a keyboard. He turned some dials. He pushed a lot of buttons.

"Is it all right?" Patrick asked.

"Yes. You'll be able to go on an adventure," Mr. Whittaker said. "Maybe I'll find out why it works for you but not for me."

"Can we go back in time?" Patrick asked. He was excited.

"How would you like to visit a Viking ship?" Mr. Whittaker asked.

Patrick and Beth thought for a moment. Patrick didn't know much about Viking ships. Beth knew a little about Viking explorers, but that was all.

"The Vikings had swords, right?" Patrick asked.

"They sure did," Mr. Whittaker said. He turned to Beth. "Is visiting a Viking ship okay with you, Beth?"

Beth didn't care about swords. But being on a Viking ship sounded great.

"Sure," she said. "I've always wanted to see the ocean."

"Let's go!" Patrick said.

"Not so fast," Mr. Whittaker said. "You have to be dressed for Viking times."

Patrick looked at his blue jeans and dinosaur T-shirt. He looked at Beth's bright pink shorts and top.

"Oh," Patrick said. "The Vikings would probably notice we didn't fit in."

"And you might get cold and wet," Mr. Whittaker said.

Mr. Whittaker walked over to the workshop wall. He opened two large sliding doors. Beyond them was another room. It was filled with rack after rack of costumes.

Mr. Whittaker chose an armful of clothes. He gave them to Beth. He gave another armful to Patrick. "You can use the changing rooms."

The cousins went to two small rooms the size of closets. They changed into the costumes. Beth came out first.

She was wearing a long white dress. On top was a long green tunic. Two brooches were pinned at the shoulders. The tunic was neatly tied with a leather belt. Her animal-skin boots came up to her knees.

"I feel like I'm in a fairy tale," Beth said. "It's fun to dress up."

"Take this, too," Mr. Whittaker said.

He gave Beth a small cloth sack. She opened it up and looked inside.

The sack was full of chess pieces. They were carved out of wood. Some of the pieces were white wood. The rest were painted red.

Beth tied the sack to her belt.

"Why do I need a chess set?" she asked.

Mr. Whittaker answered with a you'll-find-out smile.

Patrick came out of his changing room.

He was also dressed in a costume. He wore a simple white shirt with a vest over it. The vest was made of tan leather. His dark pants were tucked inside his boots.

"You look like a real Viking," Mr. Whittaker said. "But you need one more thing."

Mr. Whittaker handed Patrick a fuzzy bundle. It was a cape.

The cape was made from grizzly bear fur. It was silver with brown flecks. The cape looked thick and warm. Patrick put it on.

"Thank you," Patrick said. "I'm ready now. I can't wait to meet a sword-fighting Viking!"

The Note

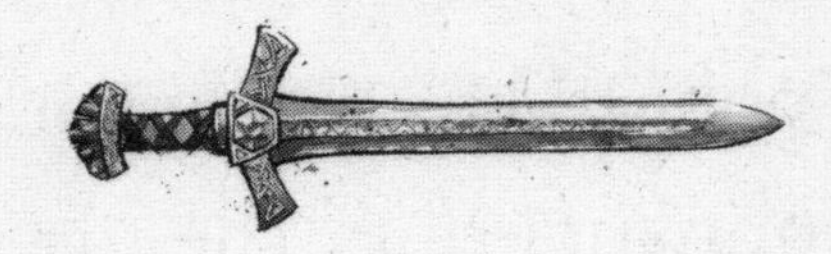

"Before you meet the Vikings," Mr. Whittaker said, "I have a small favor to ask."

"Sure! We'll do whatever you need," Beth said.

"While you're with the Vikings," Mr. Whittaker said, "find a Viking Sunstone."

"What's a Viking Sunstone?" Beth asked.

"I'm not sure—yet," Mr. Whittaker said. "I read about it in that note." He put his hand inside the machine. He pointed to the piece paper sitting on the dashboard.

Patrick and Beth noticed some things about the paper. It was thick and yellowed. It had fancy letters, and the paper looked very old.

They also noticed Mr. Whittaker's hand. He wore an unusual ring. The top was a gold square. Tiny pearls sat around the square. It was the kind of ring a king would wear.

"I found this paper inside the Imagination Station," Mr. Whittaker said.

The cousins climbed inside the machine to look at the note. They read the fancy letters:

To save Albert, I need a Viking Sunstone before the new moon. Or Lord Darkthorn will lock him inside the tower.

"Who is Albert?" Beth asked. "And what is

Lord Darkthorn's tower?"

"I'll explain all that later," Mr. Whittaker said.

"But what if we don't find the Sunstone?" Beth asked.

"Then I'll figure out a new plan," Mr. Whittaker said. "Don't worry about it. Just have a good time while you're looking."

"I just want to meet the Viking who has the Sunstone," Patrick said.

He swung an imaginary sword in the air. *Slash! Jab!*

"I think you're ready," Mr. Whittaker said. He stepped back and took his hand out. Beth noticed that the ring on his finger seemed to disappear.

"You'll be going back one thousand years," Mr. Whittaker said.

"How will we return to 'now'?" Beth asked.

"The red button will appear when you are ready to come home," Mr. Whittaker said. "Get back to where you landed. Push the button and—presto!—you'll be right back here."

Mr. Whittaker stepped away from the Imagination Station. He pushed a button on the side. The door slid closed.

Patrick looked at the control panel. The red button was flashing in the middle. He pushed it.

The Imagination Station started to shake. Then it rumbled. It seemed to move forward.

Beth gasped. She shut her eyes tight. It felt like a roller coaster that was out of control.

Patrick felt as if he were an astronaut in

a spaceship. He leaned back, waiting for takeoff.

Then the rumble grew louder.

The machine whirled.

Suddenly, everything went black.

The Tidal Wave

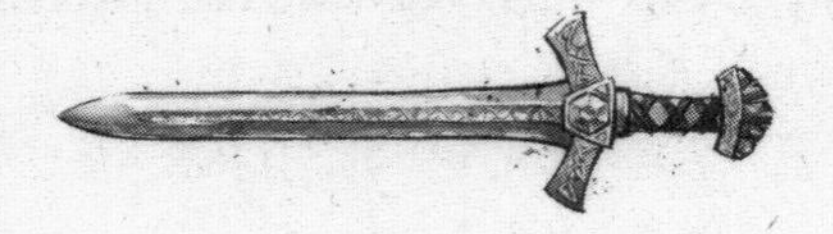

Beth opened her eyes. She saw bright green water. Tall mountains of white ice with a purple glow loomed over and around her. The ice sparkled in the sun.

Beth was dazzled by the beautiful colors.

Patrick was not.

“Where are the Vikings?” Patrick asked. “And what’s with all the ice?”

“I think we’re near the North Pole,” said Beth. “Those are icebergs.”

Beth looked away from the scenery. She and Patrick were still in the Imagination Station. But she couldn't see Whit's End anymore.

The Imagination Station appeared to be in a ship. An empty wooden ship at sea.

The ship was long and narrow. The shape reminded Beth of a giant canoe.

Beth got out of the machine and took a deep breath. She looked over the side of the boat.

"The air smells salty," Beth said. "But the water is calm. I'd say we're on an ocean inlet."

"What's that?" Patrick asked.

"A long, narrow waterway," she said.

Patrick also stepped out of the machine. Right after he did, the machine faded out of sight. It disappeared.

"Wow," Beth said.

"That's so cool!" Patrick said.

Patrick turned his thoughts to the Viking ship. He imagined it full of Vikings.

"I bet this ship could hold a bunch of Vikings," he said. "Plus all their stuff."

Patrick looked out across the water. There was only one place to get to shore. It was very far away.

"Oh, no. There are no oars," Patrick said. "We can't row to shore."

"We'd better get there somehow," said Beth. "I don't want to just sit here."

Suddenly a black shadow passed under the ship. They watched it approach a large piece of floating ice. Then a huge white animal shot out of the water. A polar bear!

The white bear stood on the floating piece of ice. It spread its front legs wide. It bared its teeth at the cousins and roared.

RAAARRRHHH!

The sound echoed off the ice.

The cousins shivered.

"Do polar bears eat kids?" Patrick asked.

"I—I don't know," said Beth.

Another black shadow passed under the ship. The cousins stepped back. They were afraid of another polar bear. But this time a seal popped its head up at them. It looked at them with jet-black eyes. Then it went under the water again.

The bear growled. It leaped into the water headfirst. The cold water splashed Beth and Patrick.

From a distance came a loud *CRAAACK!*

The sound startled them. They looked up. The top part of a large iceberg broke loose. It was the size of a small house. It hit the water with a *whump! splash!*

The impact created a huge wave.

"Hold on!" Beth shouted.

The wave curled higher and higher. The crest of the wave lifted the Viking ship and carried it away.

The ship moved fast. The prow crashed through the water.

Patrick stood at the front of the ship cheering.

"Oh, yeah!" Patrick shouted. "Keep the wave rolling!"

At first Beth was afraid. Then she was caught by the thrill of the ride. The rush of the wind chapped her cheeks. The spray of water tingled her skin.

The wave settled. The ship drifted near a rock jetty.

"Get ready to jump," said Patrick.

Patrick stood on the edge of the ship. Then he leaped across to the jetty.

"Come on, Beth," he shouted.

Beth looked at the jetty. From the ship to the rocks was farther than she had ever jumped.

"Beth, hurry," Patrick said. "The ship is drifting away now."

Beth jumped. Her front foot reached the jetty. Her second foot did not. Her boot slipped off the wet rocks. She started to fall backward.

Patrick grabbed hold of her arm and pulled Beth to safety.

"Thanks," Beth said. She was glad to be on solid ground again.

"Race you to the top of that hill!" Patrick said.

The cousins ran across the jetty to a sloping open field. They dashed up the hill. The ground was rocky. The grass was thick and bushy. Tiny purple and yellow flowers bloomed in small clumps.

Suddenly the cousins heard the clomp of hooves. They stopped running and listened.

The noise grew louder. It sounded like thunder.

A herd of reindeer crested the hill from the other side. About thirty huge brown animals charged onto the field.

The two reindeer in front had black faces. Their antlers were brown with sharp points.

And the reindeer were headed straight for the cousins.

The Spear

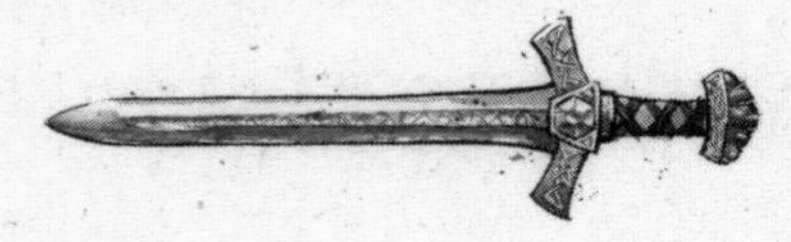

Beth froze with fear. All she could do was stare at the sharp antlers.

Patrick's heart all but stopped. The animals were coming too fast. There were so many of them. It would be useless to run.

Whoosh! A spear came flying through the air.

Thud! It landed right in front of Patrick.

"Where did that come from?" Patrick shouted.

"Who cares?" Beth shouted back at him.

"Use it!"

Patrick pulled the spear out of the ground. He moved in front of Beth. He turned the spear sideways and faced the animals.

"Out of the way!" he shouted to the coming reindeer.

He waved the spear to his left. Then to his right.

The animals did not change their path. They charged straight at the cousins.

"Whoa!" he shouted louder.

Beth was sure they'd be trampled. She closed her eyes.

"Yaw!" Patrick shouted.

He braced himself for impact.

At the last second, the lead reindeer swerved to the right. But the animals were still close.

Beth could smell them. She could feel their heat. She breathed in to make herself as thin as possible. One wrong step or stumble and she and Patrick would be crushed.

The herd thundered past in seconds. Patrick closed his eyes in relief.

"Phew!" he said. "That was close."

As soon as he opened his eyes, he saw two men on black horses. They galloped down the hill.

"Look," Beth said. "I think those

men were hunting the reindeer. One of them must have thrown the spear."

The men wore tan tunics. Their capes were red. Their helmets were gold. One held a long bow. The other clutched a sword.

"They're Vikings!" Patrick said. "I got my wish!"

Erik the Red

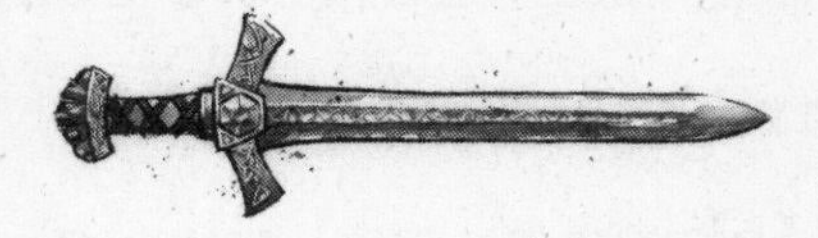

The reindeer were now forgotten. The cousins had new worries.

The two Viking men rode up close and got off their horses.

Patrick studied them. They were very tall. One was older and had red hair, *lots* of red hair. It hung to his shoulders. He also had a bushy beard. Even the skin on his face was red from the sun and wind. The other man was younger with blond hair and fair skin.

Beth thought the younger Viking was handsome. The older one looked fierce.

The hunters slowly moved to the cousins. The younger one put an arrow in his bow. He pulled back the string. He pointed the arrow at Patrick.

The elder Viking moved even closer. He lifted his sword. Patrick noticed there was a bright yellow stone on the handle.

Beth spoke out of the side of her mouth. "Drop the spear," she said quietly.

"What?" Patrick said.

"Drop the spear," Beth said again. "They think we are enemies."

Patrick had forgotten about the spear. He looked down at it. The tip was made of an animal tusk. And it was pointed straight at the men. He let the spear fall to the grass.

At once the younger Viking lowered his bow. But the older Viking kept hold of the sword.

The older red-haired Viking looked at Patrick. His mouth curved in a half smile. He turned to the younger Viking.

"The boy prisoner has shown great courage," the Red Viking said. He was talking as if the cousins couldn't hear him.

"The boy had no fear of the reindeer," he said. "He must be Norse—a Viking. He has the light hair."

The Red Viking studied Beth for a moment. He did not seem pleased.

"The girl prisoner is small and dark haired," the man said. "She has the look of a house slave."

Beth frowned. She wanted to protest. But

she was too shocked to speak.

"Who are you?" Patrick asked.

The Red Viking looked at Patrick. "I am Erik the Red," he said. He made a fist with his hand and thumped his chest twice.

Patrick didn't recognize the name. But Beth did. She gasped.

"You're the ruler of Greenland!" she said.

Erik nodded. Then he said proudly, "This is my son Leif."

He nodded toward the blond Viking. The younger man now came closer.

"You are trespassing on our land," Leif said.

"We are?" Patrick asked.

Erik looked around. "Where is your ship?" he asked. "Where are your oarsmen hiding?"

Erik leaned in closer. The children could

smell his breath. It smelled of fish and salt.

"Did the king of Norway send you to spy on us?" Erik said. "Tell me the truth. Or you will feel the blade of my sword!"

Patrick didn't know what to say. He had no idea if Norway had a king. He didn't even know where Norway was. His mouth was dry. His heart was pounding.

Beth's eyes grew large as saucers. Erik the Red was famous for fighting. No words would come out of her mouth. She couldn't breathe.

Finally Leif spoke up.

"Father," he said, "they are but children."

The older Viking took a step back and turned toward his son.

"Ha! Children are the best spies, I say!" Erik said.

Leif laughed kindly. "But they are also Christians," he said.

Erik looked surprised. "Oh?"

"Look closely," Leif said. "The girl wears the sign of the cross. See the brooches at her shoulders?"

Beth looked down at her brooches. She hadn't paid much attention to them before. They were gold and round. Each one had a cross in the center.

"The boy also wears it," Leif said.

The clasp to Patrick's bearskin cape was silver. It was shaped like a kite. The cross was in the center.

Erik grunted in anger. He reached out and stroked the fur on Patrick's cape.

"Give me the silver-skinned cape," Erik said to Patrick. "Since I am the ruler here, it belongs to me."

Patrick's hands shook as he reached to undo the clasp.

"No, Father," Leif said. "Please let the boy keep his cape. They are Christians. I will defend their rights."

Erik glared at his son. He spat on the ground. "You are too soft and kind. Why can't you be more like a Viking?"

"Always using a sword? Stealing?" Leif asked. "I will not just take what I want. Or kill for it. I am an honest trader."

"Honest?" Erik said. He sneered. And then he shook his sword at Leif. The yellow stone on its handle sparkled in the sunlight.

He shouted, "You cheated me! I sent you to Norway to trade goods. But you brought home a new God! The God of the cross!"

"Jesus the Christ," Leif said.

Leif looked at his father. The son's face was full of concern and hurt. Beth thought that this must be an old argument between them.

Erik spat on the ground again. "Your Christ is a God of peace—not war! He has no place in Greenland!"

Erik shook his sword one last time. Then he seemed to give up. He slid his weapon into its holder. He turned on his heel, walked over to his horse, and climbed on.

"You may watch over these children," Erik said to Leif. "But if I ever find them alone, I will take them as slaves!"

The Church

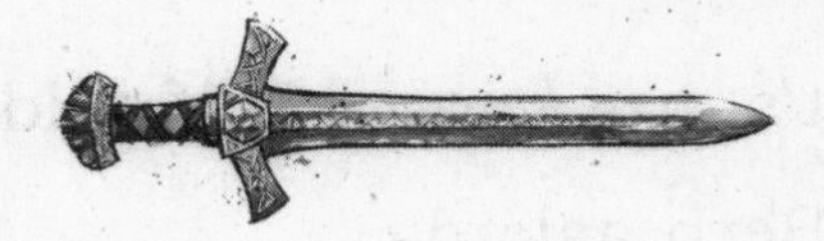

Erik had no more to say to Leif or the cousins. He jerked the horse's reins. Then he rode toward the shore.

All was still for a moment.

Then Leif turned to the children.

"You'll be safer in the village," he said. "I know where you can stay out of his way."

"Will your father really make us his slaves?" Patrick asked.

"Yes," Leif said. "But don't worry. Father

and I sail for Norway tomorrow."

"Are you sailing on that ship?" Beth asked. She pointed toward the ship she and Patrick had found. Erik the Red was now standing on the jetty.

"Yes. That's our *knorr*," Leif said.

"Knorr?" Beth asked.

"Our trading ship," Leif said. "My father is going to make sure it won't leak. Now, let's go. I have much to do today."

He lifted Beth and then Patrick onto his horse. Beth sat in front. Patrick was in the middle, and Leif was at the back. There was just enough room on the horse for the three of them.

Beth had always wanted a horse. She stroked its black mane. The hair was rough and it tickled her fingers.

The horse carried them over the hill and down into a valley. Beth had been glad to see the ocean. She had seen reindeer up close. But now she was seeing a third awesome sight: Before her was a charming Norse village.

All the houses were made of stone. They had dirt roofs with grass growing on top. Goats and sheep roamed about grazing. Others drank at a nearby stream. Large gray rocks dotted the landscape.

Leif brought the horse to a halt. They were beside a small building.

"This is the church," he said. "My father will not come inside it. Not even to harm you."

Leif helped Beth and Patrick slide off the horse. The cousins entered through a low, narrow door. Inside was one room. It was the size of Beth's bedroom back home. A rock with a cross carved on it hung from one wall. There were no windows.

In the middle of the floor sat a small fire ring. But no fire was burning. Along the walls were several wood benches.

Leif asked the cousins to wait. He left and closed the door. The cousins sat on one of the benches.

"Did you hear Leif ?" Beth asked. "The ship—the ship with the Imagination Station—is leaving tomorrow!"

Patrick sighed.

"I hadn't thought of that," he said.

"We have to find the Sunstone. We must get back to the ship before it leaves," Beth said.

"Did you see Erik's sword?" Patrick asked.

"Yeah," Beth said. "And he's not afraid to

use it. We have to stay away from him."

"Who is he?" Patrick asked.

"Erik the Red discovered this land. He named it Greenland," Beth said. "Before that he lived in Iceland."

"Why did he leave Iceland?" Patrick asked.

"A powerful man stole Erik's family treasures," Beth said. "There was a fight between the families, and people died. The Icelanders wanted the fighting to stop. So they kicked Erik out."

"They kicked him out of his own country?" said Patrick.

"Yes," Beth said. "Erik had a ship and crew. So he sailed away to become a trader. That's when he discovered Greenland. He settled here and raised a family."

"I've heard of Leif," Patrick said. "My

teacher said he discovered North America 500 years before Columbus did!"

Just then the door opened and a woman came in. She was dressed much like Beth, except a scarf covered her blonde hair.

A string of colorful beads hung between the brooches on her tunic. A large gold cross dangled from the string.

Beth was relieved to see the cross. A Christian Viking was a peaceful Viking. At least she hoped so.

"Children," she said, "I am Thjodhild, the wife of Erik the Red and mother of Leif."

Beth tried to say her name, but it sounded all wrong. It came out half birdcall, half cough.

The woman laughed.

"You may call me Hilda. That is easier to

say," she said.

Beth stood and gave Hilda a curtsey.

"I'm Beth," she said. "And this is my cousin Patrick."

Patrick said nothing. Beth gently elbowed him in the ribs. Sometimes she had to remind Patrick of his manners.

He jumped to his feet.

"Oh, hi, I guess," Patrick said. He held out his hand for a handshake. Hilda gave him a funny look.

Vikings must not know about handshakes, Patrick thought. He pulled back his hand.

"Wait," Hilda said.

She stepped outside. A minute later she came back with two soapstone bowls of milk. She put them down on a bench. She left again and came back with two plates of cooked meat.

"These are for you," she said.

The cousins thanked her.

She gave them a smile and nodded.

"I'm sorry I can't stay longer," she said.

Hilda left them. Beth and Patrick sat down again. They each said a silent prayer of thanks to God before they ate.

The milk was warm but still tasty. The meat was salty and full of juice. It had an odd taste.

Halfway through the meal, Beth stopped chewing.

"What kind of meat is this?" she asked.

"I don't know," Patrick said. He took another bite.

"Seal meat? Walrus? Reindeer?" she asked.

Patrick laughed. "Meat is meat."

She swallowed and pushed the rest of her food toward Patrick. "Then you can eat it," she said.

And he did. Beth paced around the room. Leif's ship would leave soon. They had less than a day to find a Viking Sunstone. But searching the village wouldn't be easy. They needed a plan. A safe plan.

The Ship

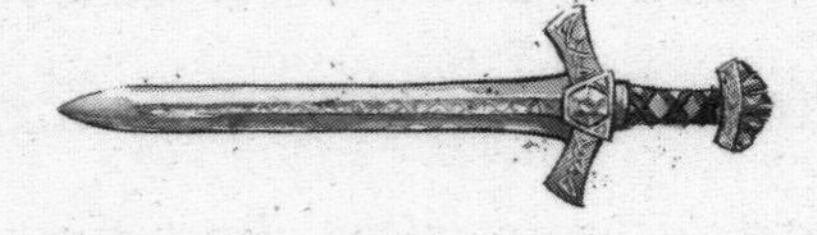

Patrick finished his meal and stood up.

"Come on," he said. "We've got to leave the church. The Sunstone isn't in here."

"Are you nuts?" Beth said. "I think we should wait for Leif. We can't go out alone. If Erik finds us—"

"If Erik finds us," Patrick said, "he'll lock us up. What's the difference? Aren't we locked up now?"

Patrick's way of thinking didn't sound

right to Beth.

"But—" she said.

"And what about Mr. Whittaker's friend?" Patrick said. "*He's* going to be locked in a tower if we don't find the Sunstone. Remember the note? 'To save Albert, I need a Viking Sunstone before the new moon. Or he will be locked inside Lord Darkthorn's tower.' "

Beth shook her head. "I want to help. But it's too dangerous. I'm staying here."

She crossed her arms.

"Okay," Patrick said. "See you when I get back."

The door closed behind him with a thud.

Patrick stepped into the sunlight. He blinked.

There were two dozen or so Viking men

marching on a path.

Four of them carried a long wood beam. It was wrapped in ropes. Patrick guessed it might be the ship's mast. It would hold up the sail.

The rest of the men carried small wooden chests or barrels on their shoulders. Bundles were tucked under their arms. Oars were strapped to their backs.

Patrick watched the crowd. Erik the Red was not among them.

"Excuse me," Patrick said to one of the men. "Where is Leif?"

"He's at the shore," the man said. "He's getting the ship ready. Isn't that what a good captain does?"

"And Erik the Red?" Patrick asked.

"He's gone home," said the man. "He says

he hurt his shoulder. But if you ask me, he's afraid to sail. He's too old."

Patrick looked at all the stuff going to the ship. What if a Sunstone were in one of the chests? Since Erik wasn't around, Patrick felt brave. He would go to the ship. He had to take the risk.

The man tossed a bundle to Patrick.

"Here," said the man, "carry this for me."

The bundle was a bedroll made of reindeer skin. Patrick walked with the Norsemen the half mile to shore.

The Viking ship was very close to the land now. A long plank of wood stretched from the ship's side to the shore. The plank had ropes tied to it so it wouldn't move.

Leif shouted orders for the sailors to load the ship. Patrick stayed at the end of the line. He didn't want Leif to see him.

He scanned the ship for Erik. The sailor had been right. The old Viking wasn't there.

The men who carried the mast walked up the plank first. Then the other men took chests, bundles, and barrels aboard. The cargo was neatly stowed in rows. The oars were laid next to the sides of the ship. Patrick followed, glad he had a bundle to carry. As long as he was helping, the men seemed to accept him.

Soon most of the men gathered to set up the mast. A group was using ropes to raise the sail. Others were placing braces around the beam.

No one was near Patrick. Now was his chance. He looked over more of the bundles. They were all just bedrolls. Some had extra

clothes inside. No Sunstone.

Patrick opened a few of the chests. Some were full of grain. Others had dried fish. He opened the largest one.

It was full of animal furs. Sheep's wool. Polar bear skins. Walrus hides. Nothing that looked like a Sunstone was inside.

He began to wonder.

All this time I've been on the ship, he thought. *But there is no sign of the Imagination Station. Where is that red button? Is the machine broken? Does Beth have to be with me?*

Then a sudden noise broke into his thoughts.

"Stop, thief!" a sailor shouted.

The Thief

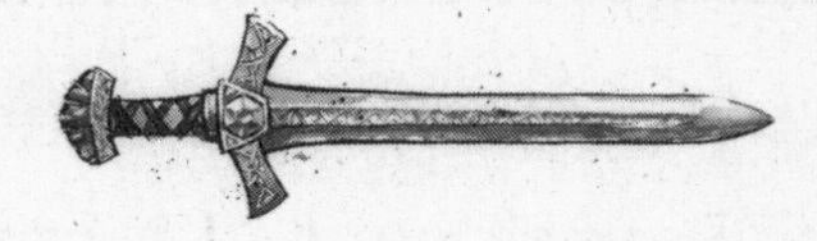

Patrick looked up from the chest of furs.

Everyone was staring at Patrick.

"Captain," said the sailor, "a boy is stealing furs!"

The sailor came up to him. He grabbed the edge of Patrick's silver cape.

"Look," he said. "He stole this fur cape."

"It's not what you think," Patrick said. "This is mine!"

The men gathered around. Some of them

pulled out knives.

"Wait," said a voice. Leif pushed through the crowd.

The sailor took a step back from Patrick.

Relief washed over Patrick. He looked up at Leif.

"I'm sorry," Patrick said. "I just wanted to see what was inside. I didn't take anything. I promise!"

Leif said to his sailors, "I'll deal with the boy. The day's work is done. You may all go. But be here before dawn tomorrow!"

A cheer went up among the men. They ran down the plank to shore.

"Where is the girl?" Leif asked Patrick. "Is she safe?"

"I left her at the church," Patrick said.

"Where *you* should be," Leif said. "Don't

you understand what will happen now?"

"No," Patrick said.

"The people are going to the last feast before we sail," Leif said.

"Great!" Patrick said. "I love parties."

"This party is not for you. They worship the Norse gods like Thor. They offer sacrifices."

Patrick gasped. "Idol worship?" he asked.

Leif frowned at him. "That is why I wanted you and the girl to stay inside the church. It's the only place you'll be safe."

Patrick took a deep breath. What if Beth had left the church? What if Erik caught her and took her to the ceremony?

"We have to go back to Beth!" he said. "Hurry!"

Patrick raced from the boat and back to

the village. Leif followed close behind. They reached the church. Patrick threw open the door.

"Beth!" he shouted.

But there was no answer.

The Feast

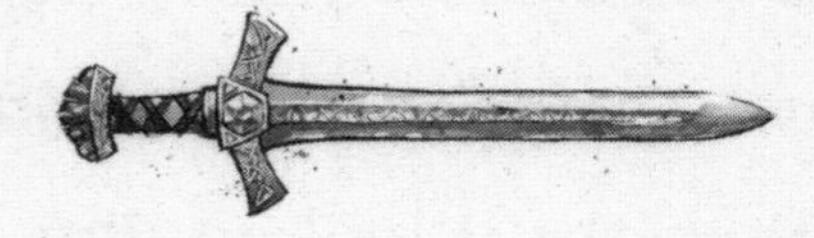

“Come with me to the longhouse,” Leif said to Patrick. “The feast will be held there. Maybe someone took her inside.”

They ran across the village. The longhouse was much larger than the church. Patrick stuck his head through the doorway and looked around. The big room was filled with men and women. A gray haze hung like fog. It was hard for Patrick to see.

He coughed and wondered what caused

the smoke. Then he saw a fire blazing in a fire ring. It was at the center of the room. Some of the smoke escaped through a small hole in the roof. But most of the smoke filled the room. No one seemed to notice.

Patrick saw a huge metal pot hanging over the fire. He thought it looked like a witch's cauldron.

The Norsemen and Norsewomen sat on long wooden benches. They ate roasted fish and meat, and they drank from wooden cups.

A group of men played bone pipes and wood drums. Young teen boys and girls sang happy songs. Others danced nearby.

Patrick moved slowly among the crowd. He searched for Beth.

A few men were playing board games. Erik

the Red was playing a game against another man. Next to Erik was Hilda. Next to Hilda was *Beth.*

Patrick couldn't believe it. There she was, sitting on a bench.

A small crowd moved in to watch Erik and the man play.

Beth saw Patrick and came over to him.

"What are you doing here?" Patrick asked.

"After you left, Hilda came to the church to check on me," Beth whispered. "Erik was with her."

"What happened?" Patrick asked.

"Erik ordered me to help cook," Beth said. "He wants me to learn to be a house slave. That way he can sell me for more money."

"But you're not cooking now," Patrick said.

"Hilda got upset," Beth said. "Erik isn't

afraid of any man. But he's afraid of Hilda. She said she would keep me safe. I've been next to her ever since."

"What game is Erik playing?" Patrick asked.

"Chess. It's his favorite game," Beth said. "But no one likes to play him."

"Why not?" Patrick asked.

"Because they're afraid of what he'll do if he loses," she said.

Patrick pointed to Erik's sword. The yellow jewel in the handle gleamed. "I think that might be the Sunstone. But I wish I could get a closer look."

"I wouldn't try," Beth said.

Suddenly Erik slapped the table. Patrick and Beth jumped. The chess pieces bounced around on the board.

"Checkmate!" he shouted.

The man who lost stood up, bowed, and walked away.

"Who will play me next?" Erik shouted.

No one answered.

He stood up and looked around. He saw Patrick. As he stared at Patrick's cape, his eyes narrowed.

"Do you play, boy?" Erik asked Patrick.

"No, sir," Patrick said.

"What about you?" Erik asked Beth.

"Y-yes," she said.

Patrick was surprised.

"You do?" he asked.

Beth opened the small sack Mr. Whittaker

had given her. She dumped the red and white chess pieces onto the table.

Erik picked up the colored pieces. They seemed bright compared to the plain pieces he used.

"Sit down!" Erik said.

"But I don't think I'm good enough to play a grown-up," Beth said.

"Sit down!" Erik said. It was an order.

Beth obeyed and sat across from him. She looked scared.

"A wager for our game," Erik said. "If I win, I will get the boy's silver cape."

"What does she get if she wins?" Patrick asked.

"You may keep your lives!" Erik said.

The people in the crowd laughed.

Hilda stood up.

"That's not fair, my husband," she said. "If she wins, she should get something."

Erik groaned. "You are too kind to slaves. What does the girl want?"

Beth looked helpless.

"I don't know," she said.

Patrick cleared his throat loudly. Beth looked at him. Patrick tilted his head toward Erik's sword.

"Oh, I know," Beth said. "If *you* win, you get the silver cape. If *I* win, I get your sword."

The crowd suddenly went quiet.

Erik looked puzzled. "My sword?"

"Child," Hilda said kindly, "that sword is a family treasure."

"What would you do with this sword?" Erik asked. "It's too big for you."

"I would keep it to remember you by," Beth said.

Erik smiled. It seemed as if he liked to be liked.

Patrick stepped forward. He said to Erik, "If you're afraid you'll lose..."

"Lose? I never lose!" Erik said.

He pounded the table with his fist. He

leaned toward Beth.

"I accept your challenge," he said.

Patrick watched as the pieces were arranged. Beth used the white ones. Erik used the red ones. Her hands looked very small compared to the Viking's.

The game lasted a long time. Patrick paced. He saw Leif watching them closely.

Erik was a smart player. But so was Beth.

After an hour, only nine pieces were left on the board.

Beth had three pawns, a bishop, and her king. Erik had one pawn, a rook, his queen, and his king.

"We can stop now," Erik said to Beth. "You can see that I have better pieces than you do. The cape is as good as mine."

"We'll see," Beth said.

Erik picked up his queen. He plunked it down near Beth's king.

"Check," he said.

Erik then looked at Patrick.

"Give me the silver cape, boy," he said.

Patrick frowned. He began to take off the cape.

"Wait, Patrick," Beth said. "Not so fast."

She picked up a pawn. It was the smallest and weakest piece on the board. She moved it one space forward. The move blocked Erik's queen.

"Checkmate," she said.

Erik glared at the board.

"How did you do that?" he roared.

Hilda laughed.

"She has also trapped you," she said, "with a little pawn."

"She must have cheated!" he shouted. "I cannot be beaten by a little girl!"

The crowd shrank back from him. They were afraid of what he might do.

Hilda put a hand on his shoulder.

"My husband, the girl won fairly," she said calmly.

Erik stood up. His face turned a deep red with anger.

"No!" he howled.

He pulled his sword out of the holder. Arm straight, he held it in the air. His arm started to tremble with rage.

"Remember your honor," Hilda said softly.

Bam! Erik threw the sword down on the table. He then turned and pushed through the crowd.

One by one the Vikings around the game

table left. Most of them followed Erik to the fire ring. The musicians began to play again.

Beth thought it would feel good to beat Erik. But she felt sad as she put the chess pieces back in her sack. Winning the sword didn't seem right somehow.

Leif came over to them. "That was a risky thing to do. What will you do with the sword?"

"It isn't for us to keep," Patrick said.

"Oh?" Leif said. He lifted an eyebrow in surprise.

"Though I always wanted a sword," Patrick said.

And this one was beautiful. He picked it up from the table. It was heavy. He looked at the jewel. Mr. Whittaker would be so pleased to see it. He then used both hands to slide the sword into his belt.

Hilda came up behind the cousins. She put one hand on each of their shoulders.

"It's time for us to leave," she said.

"You have warned the other Christians?" Leif asked her.

She nodded.

"Warned them about what?" Beth asked.

"The sacrifices to the gods are about to begin," Hilda replied.

Beth and Patrick turned to look at the fire ring. Many of the Viking men and women were now dancing around it. Cups were in their hands. They threw liquid on the fire.

"What are they doing?" Beth asked Leif.

"They are throwing beer onto the fire," Leif said, "as a sacrifice to a false god."

The fire hissed and flared. The yellow light

cast a strange glow on everything.

A deep sadness crossed over Leif's face.

"My mother is right," he said. "This is no place for Christians—or children."

The Full Moon

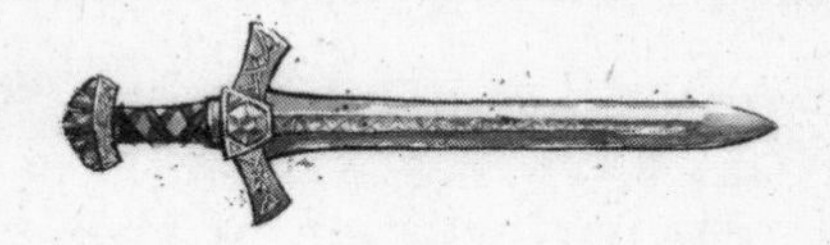

Leif, Hilda, and the cousins left the longhouse. So did a few of the men and women. As the Norse Christians walked toward their homes, they bid Leif and Hilda good night.

Beth breathed in the fresh air of the village courtyard. She looked up at the sky.

Wispy green lights danced like smoke in the wind.

"What is that?" Patrick asked.

"I've seen it on TV. It's called the Northern Lights," Beth whispered to Patrick. It was the fourth amazing thing she had seen in Greenland.

The moon was full. It cast a white glow over the village.

The moon reminded her of the note from inside the Imagination Station.

I need a Viking Sunstone before the new moon.

Beth pulled on Leif's sleeve.

"When is the new moon?" she asked.

Leif stroked his blond beard. "What manner of girl are you?" he said. "You know chess. But you don't know the new moon is in fourteen days. Come. I will show you the Sunstone. It will teach you about the sky."

Patrick and Beth both gasped.

Patrick put a hand on the hilt of the sword. “Isn’t this yellow jewel the Sunstone?”

Leif laughed.

“No,” he said. “What made you think it was?”

“Just a guess,” Patrick said sadly. “So, where is the real Sunstone?”

Leif led them to a huge rock in the center of the village. The Sunstone was taller than Beth. It had symbols, holes, and lines carved all over it.

“We use the Sunstone to mark the seasons,” Leif said. “It also points us southward.”

Leif knelt down by the rock. He took Patrick’s hand and placed it on the Sunstone.

“Feel that arrow mark?” Leif asked.

Patrick nodded.

"At noon the sun passes over at that mark," Leif said. "Then the Sunstone casts a shadow. We mark where the shadow falls here."

Leif dragged his finger across the ground.

Beth and Patrick followed his motion.

Several flat rocks surrounded the Sunstone. Symbols and holes were carved into the rocks as well.

"When the noon sun reaches these slash marks," Leif said, "we know it is spring. We can sail."

"Can the Sunstone be moved away from Greenland?" Beth asked.

Leif looked at Beth.

"Of course not," he said. "This stone will only work in this place. My people rely on it."

Beth turned to Patrick. She whispered, "Now what are we supposed to do?"

The Bolted Door

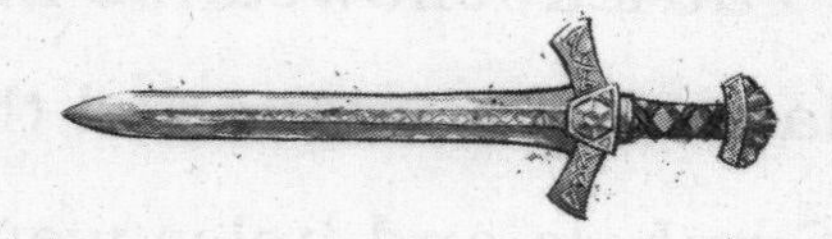

Patrick and Beth were alone in the church. Leif had already said good-bye. Hilda had helped the cousins get ready for the night. And then she, too, had left them.

A small fire burned in the fire ring. Wrapped in warm fur blankets, the cousins lay sleeping on the dirt floor.

A loud *thud* outside the door woke Beth. She had been dreaming about Albert. She dreamed he was trapped in a tall tower. He had no food. No water.

Patrick also stirred. But he was still half asleep.

"I had hoped we could help Mr. Whittaker and his friend Albert," Beth said sadly. "But we can't bring the Sunstone to Whit's End."

They were sad and silent for a while. Patrick snuggled deeper into his fur blanket. Trying to think hurt his head.

"And we have to get back to the Imagination Station," Beth said. "Otherwise the red button will sail away with Leif."

"We'll go first thing in the morning," Patrick said. "I ache all over. I'm tired."

He rolled over. His back was now toward Beth.

"No," said Beth. "We have to go now. I

have a feeling it *is* morning."

She threw the fur covers off and sat up. She put on her boots.

"Come on, Patrick," she said. "Let's see if the sun is up."

"Maybe we should stay," Patrick said. "There's no school here."

"Stay? Leif is leaving for Norway," Beth said. "Then Erik the Red will make us his slaves. He might even sell us to a farmer. Then you'd wish for school."

"I don't want to take care of sheep," Patrick said.

"And remember that we have his sword—a family treasure," Beth said. "Don't forget what happened last time someone took his treasures."

Patrick decided he wanted to be far away

from Erik. He quickly put on his boots. "Okay," he said. "I'm coming."

In a few minutes, they were ready. They went to the door. They pushed on it. They pulled on it. It wouldn't move.

"There must be a beam across the door outside," Beth said.

Patrick took the sword from his belt. "I'll whack at the door with this. Step back." He lifted the sword with both arms above his head.

Wham!

The sword made a small dent.

Wham!

Patrick swung as hard as he could.

Wham!

Beth covered her ears. "The banging is too loud. You'll wake the whole village!"

“Then what are we supposed to do?” Patrick asked. He kicked the door.

It slowly swung open.

The cousins looked at the doorway. They expected someone to step inside. No one came.

Patrick pushed the door farther open. He stepped outside.

“How did that happen?” Beth asked.

The wood beam that had locked the door was now resting against the outside wall of the church.

“Look!” Patrick said and pointed.

A man was running away from the village. Patrick saw the faint outline of a helmet on his head. He also heard the clanging of the man’s armor.

“Who is that?” Beth asked.

“I don’t know. But he’s wearing armor,”

Patrick said.

Beth looked at Patrick. “So?”

“Vikings don’t wear armor like that,” Patrick said.

Beth pushed past Patrick. “It doesn’t matter,” she said. “The sun is rising. We have to get to that ship. Or we’ll never get home.”

The Red Sail

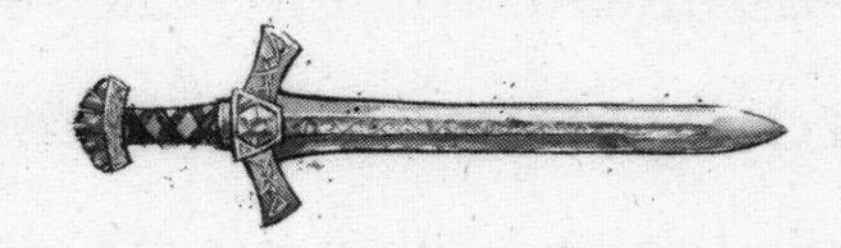

The cousins ran up the hill toward the Viking ship. Beth's dress flapped around her legs. The sword banged against Patrick's leg. They both ran slower than usual.

From the top of the hill, they saw that the ship's red sail was up. It fluttered in the breeze.

"Hurry!" Patrick said to Beth.

Beth kept her eye on the ocean. Clouds were moving in. The morning sun was now almost covered. Beth squinted to see the water. Patrick was right. The oars were down and the Viking ship was moving away from the shore.

"We can still make it!" Patrick said.

They heard the sound of hooves behind them. Patrick looked over his shoulder. This time it wasn't reindeer. A man on a horse crested the hill.

"It's Erik!" Patrick said.

"Is he after us?" Beth asked.

"I don't want to stick around to find out," Patrick said. "Run!"

Beth lifted her dress to her knees to get the cloth out of her way. She ran as fast as she could toward the jetty.

Patrick began to follow. But something inside told him to wait. He turned.

Erik was coming upon him now. They made eye contact. The Viking pulled back on the reins.

"How did you get out of the church?" Erik asked. "I bolted the door this morning."

"Someone helped us," Patrick said.

"It doesn't matter. You won't escape me," Erik said. He lifted a long spear. "You have my sword. You and the girl dishonored me in front of my people. I want revenge."

"We didn't mean to dishonor you," Patrick said. He glanced at Beth, who was now near the ship. She had run without looking back.

"I will now send you to your gods," Erik said. He drew his arm back to throw the spear.

"*God,*" Patrick said. "There's only one." As he said it, he prayed God would help him now.

At that moment, there was an

earth-shaking roar. Patrick spun around. A polar bear stood on a nearby cliff. It roared again even louder.

Erik's horse whinnied. It reared up from fear. Its front hooves waved wildly in the air.

Erik dropped the spear. He shouted as he was thrown from the horse.

Whomp!

The Viking moaned. The horse ran off.

Patrick saw his chance. He began to run. He saw that Beth had made it aboard the ship. She was shouting for him to hurry. The oars were up. But the wind had caught the sails. It was pushing the boat farther from shore.

Patrick had taken only a few steps when he heard Erik cry out.

Patrick looked back.

Erik was clutching his ankle.

"Aiii!" he said. "My foot is hurt. I can't walk."

Patrick slowly approached Erik.

"Really?" Patrick asked.

"I don't play children's games," he said. "I'm hurt!"

"I'll help you up," Patrick said.

Erik sneered and spat on the ground. "Go away, boy. I don't need *your* help. Run now, unless you are a fool."

"But I can't leave you like this," Patrick said.

"Why would you stay?" Erik said. "Unless you intend to run me through with the sword. It is what I would do if I were you."

Patrick had forgotten about the sword. He slowly drew it from his belt. He held it up. The sword was long and sharp.

Erik said, "Well? Don't be slow if you're going to kill me."

Patrick moved closer to Erik. The Viking stiffened as if waiting for death.

Then Patrick stopped. He carefully turned the weapon handle toward Erik.

Erik's eyes narrowed. "What are you doing?"

"This belongs to you," Patrick said. "It is your family treasure. It was wrong of me to take it."

"What trickery is this?" Erik asked.

"Take the sword," Patrick said. He stepped forward. "I don't want to use one anymore."

Erik pushed himself up on one knee. He reached forward and grabbed the sword. He then jabbed it in the air.

Patrick stepped back.

"You're still my prisoner," Erik said as he crawled toward Patrick. He thrust the point at Patrick. "If I hadn't hurt my foot . . ."

Patrick stayed out of Erik's reach. The old Viking dragged himself forward. He slashed at the air.

Patrick quickly looked at the ship. He was going to miss his chance to go home. Still, something inside him told him to stop. There was one more thing to do. He unclasped the silver cape and took it off.

"Take this as a gift," Patrick said.

He dropped the cape on the ground for the Viking to pick up.

"Why?" Erik said. "Why would you treat me with kindness? I would kill you if I could."

"Because the God of the cross wants me to do it," Patrick said. "I'm supposed to be kind to my enemies."

Erik glared at him. "It is fool's talk!

Kindness will lead to death—for you and all Christians!"

Patrick ignored the Viking's words. He ran with all his might to the rock jetty.

The oars were in the water again. Leif was ordering the men to fight the wind and get the boat closer to shore.

"Jump!" Beth yelled.

Patrick pushed off from the jetty with a burst of speed. He sailed through the air.

I might make it, he thought. *I might.*

But he missed.

Splash!

He fell into the icy water.

The Blue Stone

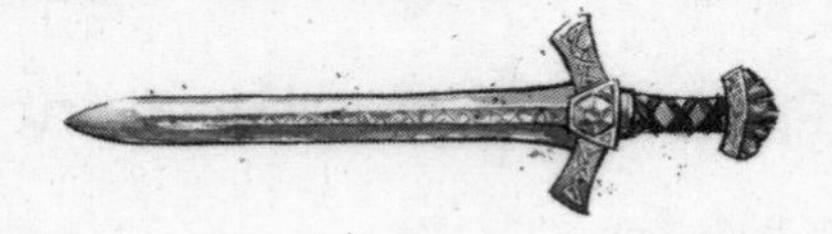

Patrick sat on the top of a wood chest. He was soaking wet. His arms ached from being pulled into the ship by an oar. His legs hurt from being scraped against the side of the ship.

Beth sat down next to him.

He looked at her. “Well?”

She shook her head. “I’ve looked over every inch of the ship. There’s no sign of the Imagination Station or a red button.”

Patrick frowned, then put his head in his hands. "This is awful. We don't have a Sunstone. We don't have a sword. And we're not going home. We're going to Norway!"

"Look at the bright side," she said. "Erik isn't on board. You are. Leif is. And Norway has a Christian king."

The ship was out on the open sea now. The day was overcast and misty. The sun was barely visible.

Patrick shivered. He really missed the silver bearskin cape now. He crossed his arms over his chest. He rubbed his arms with his fingers.

Leif saw him trying to keep warm.

"What happened to your cape?" Leif asked. "It was a fine pelt."

"I left it behind," Patrick said. He didn't

want to tell Leif he had given it to Erik.

Leif tossed him a white bundle.

"Use this blanket," he said. "It's not grand like your cape. But it's warm."

"Thanks," Patrick said. He huddled under the blanket.

"What kind of animal was that cape made from?" Leif said. "I have never seen silver fur before."

"It's from North America," Beth said. "Grizzly bears live in Canada."

"North America?" Leif asked. "Canada? Where is this place?"

Beth asked to borrow a knife. Leif handed her a small one. Its handle was made out of a reindeer antler.

Beth carved a large shape into the top of a barrel.

"This is Greenland," she said.

She marked north with an arrow pointing up. Then she drew a small circle.

"And this is Iceland," she said.

She filled in part of Europe on the right. Then she drew a huge blob to the left of Greenland.

"This is North America," she said.

She marked west by carving a sunset. She swept her hand across the top of the blob.

"This is where the silver bears come from," she said.

Next she pointed to a spot in the blob's center.

"And this," she said, "is where Patrick and I live."

"So far from the sea," Leif said. He shook his head in wonder.

He studied the map for a long while. He took back the knife and pointed to a spot on the coast of Canada.

"I had a friend who sailed along here," Leif said. "But he didn't land. I hope to visit it one day."

"You will," Beth said.

Leif closed his eyes. He stroked his beard. Then he called to his men.

"We head west," he said. "Turn the sail. We are not going to Norway. Today we sail to new lands."

Then Leif put his hand in his pants pocket. He took out a blue stone. It was very thin.

He held it up to his right eye. He looked through the stone at the horizon.

"What is that?" Beth asked.

"This stone helps me see through the clouds," he said. "It is easier to see the sun on dark days. The sun helps me find the right direction."

Patrick and Beth looked at each other.

"Is that another kind of Sunstone?" Patrick asked.

Leif put the blue stone in Patrick's hand. "Yes," he said. "We use them on our ships."

Patrick looked at the stone in his hand.

"May we have this one?" Beth asked. "I'll trade you my chess set for it."

Leif thought about it. And then he nodded. "Since I have another stone, I will accept your trade," he said. "And your chess set is a fine one. Thank you."

Beth took the small sack from her belt and handed it to him.

Suddenly the red button to the Imagination Station appeared. It was in the center of the barrel top with Beth's map.

"Look!" Patrick said.

Beth saw it and laughed. "It was right in front of us."

"What was?" Leif asked. He couldn't see the button.

Patrick reached for the button.

"Wait!" Beth said, stopping him. "We have to say good-bye."

"Good-bye?" Leif asked.

She gave Leif a quick hug. "Yes. It's time for us to leave."

Leif looked around.

"In the middle of the ocean?" he asked.

Patrick stepped forward and held out his right hand.

Leif stared at Patrick's hand. The Viking had a puzzled look on his face.

"Oh, that's right," Patrick said. "Vikings don't know about handshakes. . . . Well, good-bye then."

Patrick reached over and pushed the red button.

Suddenly, Leif, the sailors, the ship, and even the ocean disappeared.

The Second Note

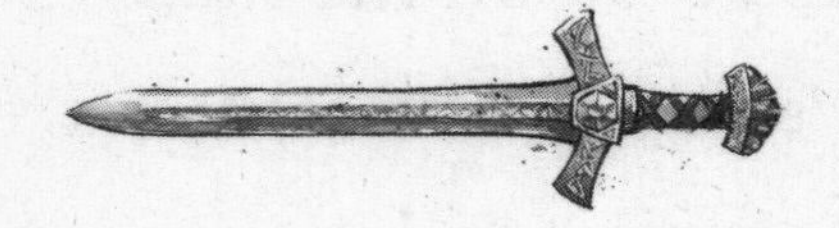

The cousins were back in the Imagination Station at Whit's End.

The door slid open, and Mr. Whittaker looked at them. "How was it?" he asked.

Patrick held up the blue stone.

"You found it!" Mr. Whittaker said. He leaned in and took the stone. "You found a real Viking Sunstone!"

"And we met Leif Eriksson—" Beth said.

"And his father, Erik the Red—" Patrick said.

"And his mother, Hilda—" Beth said.

Mr. Whittaker raised his hands.

"Whoa, slow down," Mr. Whittaker said. "Start from the beginning."

The cousins took turns telling him what had happened.

After they finished, Whit smiled. "Well done," he said.

They looked at him.

"What did we do well?" Beth asked.

"Erik the Red thought being warlike was the best way to live," Mr. Whittaker said. "Beth, you beat Erik at a game—a peaceful game. That showed Erik that Christians can win by being smart."

Beth smiled. She was pleased.

Mr. Whittaker turned to Patrick. "And Patrick," he said, "Erik was mean to you.

But you showed him kindness. That's just like God. He shows us kindness even when we don't deserve it."

Patrick's cheeks turned red.

Mr. Whittaker reached in and patted them both on the shoulders. "Well done," he said again.

Beth noticed the fancy ring on Mr. Whittaker's finger again.

Am I seeing things? she asked herself. *Why does it appear on his hand when it's in the machine? But when his hand is outside, the ring disappears. Why?*

Mr. Whittaker studied the Sunstone.

"Very interesting," Mr. Whittaker said. "What did the Vikings do with it?"

Beth told him that Leif used it to see the

sun better.

"It does something to the light on cloudy days," she said. "It makes it easier to find the sun."

"What do we do with the stone now?" Patrick asked. "How will the person who wrote the note get it?"

"Leave that to me," Mr. Whittaker said. "I think I know what to do to help Albert in time."

He set the stone on the dashboard next to the note. But wait! Suddenly a second note was next to the first one.

"Hey!" Patrick said. He pointed at the dash. "When did that show up?"

"Just now," Mr. Whittaker said. He seemed surprised.

Beth picked up the new note. She read aloud the curly letters written in black ink:

More trouble for Albert. Lord Darkthorn is angry. The Roman monk's silver cup is missing. We need it before the new moon. May God be with you.

"What does that mean, Mr. Whittaker?" Patrick asked.

Mr. Whittaker thought for a long while. He pushed at his glasses. He rubbed his nose. "I think that means another trip to Rome," Mr. Whittaker said. "Tomorrow." He gazed at them.

"Who?" Patrick asked.

"Us?" Beth said and gasped.

"Only if you want to go," Mr. Whittaker said.

"Yes!" the cousins said.

Patrick added, "Vikings one day and Rome the next! How good does it get?"

Puzzle

Do you want to solve a puzzle as Patrick and Beth did? All you have to do is finish the following sentences. Then you'll know the secret word—and the name of Leif Eriksson's God.

1. In chapter 4, Patrick and Beth jumped on to a rock [ ] ___ ___ ___ ___.

2. The Red Viking's first name was [ ] ___ ___ ___.

3. In a chess game, Beth won a [ ] ___ ___ ___ ___.

4 Beth and Patrick needed to find a Viking

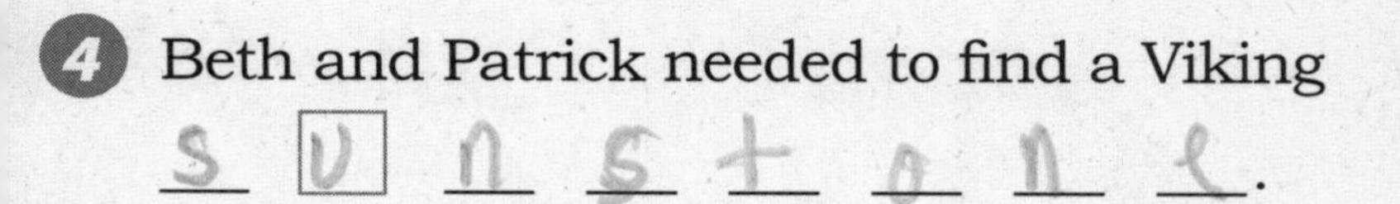

5 In chapter 11, Beth saw the Northern

Each answer has a letter in a box. Write those letters, in order, in the boxes below. The answer is the secret word:

Go to TheImaginationStation.com
Click on 'Secret Word'
Type in the answer,
and you'll receive a prize.

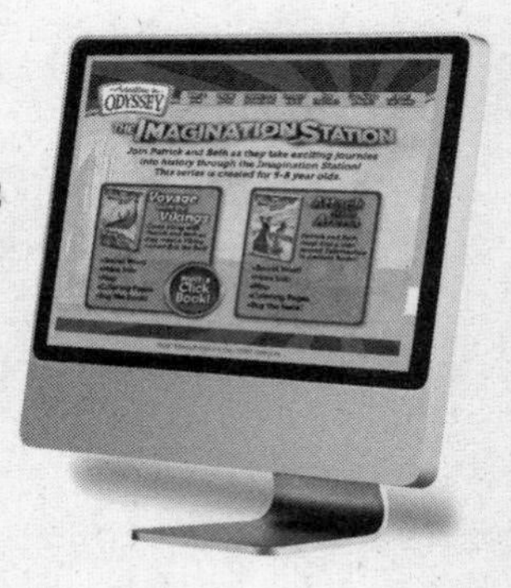

AUTHOR MARIANNE HERING is former editor of *Focus on the Family Clubhouse*® magazine. She has written more than a dozen children's books. She likes to take walks in the rain with her golden retriever, Chase.

ILLUSTRATOR DAVID HOHN draws and paints books, posters, and projects of all kinds. He works from his studio in Portland, Oregon.

AUTHOR PAUL McCUSKER is a writer and director for *Adventures in Odyssey*.® He has written over fifty novels and dramas. Paul likes peanut butter-and-banana sandwiches and wears his belt backward.